"*Amazing Annabelle and the Apple Celebration* is truly an amazing story. The story reflects on having a positive attitude towards school and the wonderful feeling a child can have because of it. More importantly, Linda Taylor shows children that a positive attitude can give you the power to change the behavior of bullying. This is a powerful lesson that children need to have. I'm looking forward to Amazing Annabelle's next adventures."

—*Cathy DeSousa, Teacher/Parent*

"Amazing Annabelle lives her family motto: 'Life is whatever you make it!' As she begins a new school year, Annabelle is determined to make it an amazing one. When she encounters a challenge, Annabelle launches Operation Kindness with surprising results. Children will enjoy the delicious characters they encounter in Amazing Annabelle, from Kindhearted Kaitlyn to Principal Johnny Appleseed. I am looking forward to Amazing Annabelle's next adventures!"

—*Deirdre Hackeling, 3rd Grade Teacher*

"Annabelle is a character full of spunk, class, and positivity. Fueled with ambitions of having an adventure-filled school year, Annabelle is excited to see what the month of September has in store. The Apple Celebration is a perfect time for Annabelle to really flaunt her fashion sense, coordinating perfectly to the theme with red apple bracelets, earrings, and dresses, but will one student turn her bubbly positivity into rotten negativity? This story really defines the value of kindness and how far one act of kindness can go."

—*Becky Tesoro, Library Media Specialist*

Amazing Annabelle

AND THE APPLE CELEBRATION

LINDA TAYLOR

ILLUSTRATED BY KYLE HORNE

Touch Point Productions & Publishing
Long Island, NY

Amazing Annabelle and the Apple Celebration
by Linda Taylor
Copyright ©2018 Linda Taylor

ISBN 978-1-947829-00-8
For Worldwide Distribution
Printed in the U.S.A.

Touch Point Productions & Publishing Inc.
Long Island, NY
amazingannabelle.com

To my countless

students—

Oh, how you've

inspired me!

Contents

1 Introducing Annabelle   *1*

2 Adventurous Plans   *12*

3 The Introduction   *18*

4 Apple Research Project   *29*

5 Problems in the Challenge   *39*

6 Pep Talk   *45*

7 Operation Kindness   *54*

8 Johnny Appleseed   *61*

9 Stepping Out of the Comfort Zone   *70*

10 Apple Celebration   *75*

The Apple Celebration

It's the start of an amazing adventure
Here at Melville Elementary School.
Annabelle is so excited,
And she always tries to dress cool.

Her mom calls her a social butterfly.
Her dad calls her a super sponge.
Annabelle has many adventurous plans.
She's ready to take the plunge.

She deals with real situations.
She acknowledges her feelings and then
Seeks different ways,
Goes into "Operation Kindness" phase.

And works through conflicts
Again and again.
Apple celebrations are fun.
The excitement has just begun!

1

INTRODUCING ANNABELLE

When Annabelle Copeland was about to go back to school in September, she was bursting at the seams with excitement. There was nothing she enjoyed more than school. Of course she liked family times, trips, and special occasions as everyone else did. However, to Annabelle, school was one of the greatest adventures in the whole wide world! It was right up there with Christmas and birthday parties.

School was a place where Annabelle could shine and show everyone just how much she knew about everything. It was also a time for her to dress up in her best clothes and be the fashion star she's always been. Most of all, it was where she learned about new and exciting things and made new friends.

Annabelle's mom always called her a social butterfly because she could hold an intelligent conversation with just about anyone, adult and kid alike. Her dad called her a super sponge because she always remembered everything that was taught in school, almost word for word. Not only was she a great listener, she also gave out pretty good advice. Annabelle's parents knew that she was a very special and amazing girl. So they started calling her Amazing Annabelle.

As Annabelle stood in front of the mirror in her room that morning, she took off her satin scarf. When it slid off her head, her beautiful curls tumbled onto her shoulders. She evaluated her hair in the mirror thinking, *What shall I do with all this hair today?* She thought back to the days when her mother fixed her hair and was suddenly inspired. She gathered her hair into a big beautiful puff and brushed the edges up. Then she secured everything together with a hair tie.

"There, now I look really amazing!" Annabelle said to herself. "But wait—" She thought for a minute. "Hmm, I think this hairstyle needs one more thing."

She pulled out a pretty red bow from her top dresser drawer and looked in the mirror while she clipped it into her hair.

"That's more like it," she said, beaming with confidence.

"Now, how will I accessorize?" she thought aloud to herself as she observed the counter. "Oh, I know," she said, as the light bulb turned on in her head.

Annabelle ran with excitement to her

jewelry box and pulled out the pretty red necklace, bracelet, and earrings set she had received for her birthday last year. Annabelle loved looking stylish wherever she went. This was just another thing that made her so amazing.

Once again she stood in front of the mirror and put on her jewelry. As she began adjusting the sleeves on her shirt, she wondered, *Should I wear my sleeves up or down—which way looks better?*

As she thought about this question, her big sister, Alice, barged into her bedroom and demanded, "Annabelle, have you seen my brush? I can't find it anywhere!"

Annabelle knew she had borrowed Alice's brush without asking and was probably going to be in big trouble. She picked up the brush off the dresser and went to the door to hand it to Alice.

"I just had to use it for a minute to get ready for school," Annabelle said.

"Next time use your own brush!" Alice replied, grabbing the brush from Annabelle. "You didn't even ask to use it!"

"I was having a 9-1-1 hair emergency! I couldn't find the brush Mom bought for me last week. And I know you wouldn't want me to go to school with my hair a mess!"

"Oh please, that's not a good excuse. I never want you to touch my things again without asking me first!" Alice ordered.

Alice had every right to be completely upset. Annabelle tried to smooth things over.

"Okay, I hear you loud and clear, and you're absolutely right. It will never happen again. But since you're in my room, do you think I should wear my sleeves up or down?" Annabelle asked.

"Who cares, Annabelle? It looks fine both ways, okay? And besides, I have more important things to worry about, such as *my* hair, which is *not* done yet, thanks to you!" Alice left the room in a hurry.

"I can't believe I'm asking her for fashion advice anyway," Annabelle whispered to herself. "Okay then, I'll wear my sleeves up," she decided and went downstairs to the kitchen.

Her family was already sitting at the table, except for Alice, who was still upstairs fixing her hair.

Annabelle's dad greeted his daughter as she sat down at the table for breakfast.

"Hello, honey, I was starting to think that I wouldn't get a chance to see you this morning on your first day of school this year," her dad said.

"Hi, Dad, you know, beauty really does

take time. And I had to make sure I was super amazing for the first day of school," Annabelle explained and started eating her breakfast.

Her little brother, Jason, looked up at her with a confused expression on his face.

"I really don't see what the big deal is about school anyway. I mean, you go into a big building, talk to some kids, listen to a teacher, and then you come home. What's the big deal?" Jason asked.

"Little kids have so much to learn. I just can't wait for you to get older and more mature, Jason," Annabelle said before taking another bite of her apple muffin.

Jason quickly stood up and put his hands on his hips. "I *am* mature, for your information, and I'll grow up when I'm good and ready!"

"Whatever, Jason, you're killing my amazing school vibe! Could you just stop talking to me?" Annabelle was clearly bothered by her brother's childish behavior.

"I'll talk to you whenever I feel like it!" Jason yelled, plopping back down in his chair.

"Will you two knock it off and finish eating your breakfast already?" Mom asked. Trying to lighten the mood, she continued, "It's a beautiful day, and I know some great things are going to happen."

"Ditto to that. On that bright note, I'm off," Dad said as he stood to his feet. "Have a great day at school, both of you!"

As he was leaving, Dad kissed them both on the head.

"Have a great day, honey," Mom said to him.

"Bye, Dad, have an amazing day!" Annabelle added and then took another bite of her apple muffin.

"Yeah, ditto to that," Jason said, laughing as he poked fun at his dad.

"Okay there, Mr. Wise Guy. I know you don't want the tickle police to come over there," Dad said, laughing.

Just then Alice hurried down the stairs in the nick of time to see her dad leave.

"Bye, Dad, have a good day!" Alice called out as she grabbed a bagel from a plate on the counter.

"Bye, honey!" replied Dad as he went out the door.

The kids were still finishing up breakfast when their mom glanced out the window and suddenly noticed something.

"Oh my! The bus is already down the street! Kids, you'll have to make a run for it!" Mom shouted.

They quickly said goodbye to their mom, picked up their backpacks, and raced for the front door. Annabelle grabbed an extra apple for her teacher and put it in her backpack as she rushed out, still finishing her apple muffin.

This has been such a crazy start to school already! I can't wait to see what happens when I actually get there! Annabelle thought as she ran towards the bus stop.

2

ADVENTUROUS PLANS

When Annabelle climbed on the bus, she was excited to see her friend Kaitlyn waving at her. She shoved the last of her apple muffin in her mouth and started looking for a seat.

"I saved you a seat!" Kaitlyn called out to her.

Annabelle sat down next to Kaitlyn, and the girls gave each other a friendly hug. Annabelle hadn't seen Kaitlyn for most of the summer because Kaitlyn had traveled with her family a lot. She had truly missed her friend.

"So, how was your summer? What cool adventures did you have this time?" Annabelle asked.

"Nothing spectacular happened this year. We just went to the same old boring places that we usually go to. You know, my grandparent's house, my aunt and uncle's house, then my mom's cousin's house, and then we went to my other grandparents' house. Plus, my annoying brother just made matters worse," said Kaitlyn, rolling her eyes at the thought of her boring summer.

Last year Kaitlyn's family went on a special trip to Disney World and couldn't stop talking about it all year long. I guess trips like that don't happen every year, Annabelle thought.

One thing Annabelle and Kaitlyn had in common is that they both liked the same things. They both also had annoying brothers who were the same age.

As they sat together on the bus, they showed each other the toy action figures they had put in their lunchboxes.

"Don't worry about your unexciting

summer," said Annabelle, "because that's all about to change. I can say with confidence that this school year is going to be the biggest adventure yet!"

"How do you figure that?" Kaitlyn asked with a hint of doubt in her voice.

"My dad says that life is whatever you make of it. So, if you want school to be adventurous and exciting, you have to make it that way," Annabelle said.

"How do we do that?" Kaitlyn was still not sure.

"First, you need a positive attitude," Annabelle said.

"What does that mean?"

"It means we have to have a go-getter spirit this year, and we need more confidence in ourselves. We need to make changes and events happen in our life and in our school."

Kaitlyn was surprised by her friend's stirring speech.

"So, I guess you're going to be running for class president at some point in the school year too," Kaitlyn said and rolled her eyes.

Annabelle didn't notice her friend's sarcasm. "Hmm," she said, "that's not a bad idea." Annabelle thought about it some more as the bus neared the school and told Kaitlyn they should give it a try.

Kaitlyn had meant her idea as a joke, but since Annabelle was one of her best friends, she was willing to give it a shot.

"So, what's our first move?" Kaitlyn asked.

"Well, I think we should set a positive tone early. We should be extra friendly to everyone and volunteer for things around the classroom," Annabelle said.

"So, are you saying that we should become teacher's pets?" Kaitlyn asked. She wasn't so sure about that one.

"Well, we don't want to overdo it, but we can certainly be two outstanding and amazing students."

"I think I can do that," said Kaitlyn, smiling. "I mean, we already are *so* very wonderful already."

"I like the way you're thinking now!" Annabelle smiled. "Who knows, maybe our teacher will even let us make some decisions for the class!" Annabelle was getting excited about the possibilities.

Annabelle and Kaitlyn continued sharing their many ideas until the bus reached Melville Elementary School.

3

THE INTRODUCTION

Just as expected, Annabelle and Kaitlyn were in the same class once again. They had been in the same class together since preschool. Their new teacher seemed very friendly and funny. She reminded Annabelle of a familiar television character who was full of energy.

Their teacher gave each student a name tag to wear so that she could memorize their names easier. As everyone settled in their seats, she introduced herself.

"Hello, class! My name is Mrs. Mitchell and I'm new to this school. We're going to have an amazing school year, and I always welcome class participation. We're going to start this morning off by having everyone introduce themselves and share three important things about themselves. Now, who wants to go first?" Mrs. Mitchell asked, beaming with excitement.

Annabelle and Kaitlyn's hands shot up almost immediately, along with two other students, Sally and Barry. Mrs. Mitchell called on Sally first.

Annabelle knew Sally since kindergarten. She remembered her clearly as one of the mean girls who pushed her down on the playground two years ago. The monitor had made Sally apologize, but unfortunately the two never truly made up or became good friends.

"Hi, my name is Sally," she began. "Three important things about me are that I love to play on the playground, I love to play with my toys at home, and I love to play soccer and kick the ball."

Annabelle immediately began to think about how physical two of her choices were. She wondered if Sally remembered pushing her down on the playground two years ago.

Then she thought about how her mom told her that it's not good to hold on to bad feelings about someone. She should leave the past behind her.

Annabelle quickly turned her attention to Barry, who was chosen next. She really liked Barry. They lived on the same block, and their parents had always been close friends. Annabelle remembered the time when she went swimming in his pool that summer. Her thoughts were interrupted as he introduced himself.

"Three important things about me are that I love to build Lego buildings, I love to eat macaroni and cheese, and I love to swim in my pool."

Annabelle could relate to his last two choices because she loved doing those things too. But she considered the importance of choices in general, thinking carefully about what she would share with the class. Was making a Lego building or eating food or swimming really that important or impressive?

Kaitlyn was chosen next. Her description of herself was short and sweet. "The three most important things about me are my family, my friends, and my future," she said.

Annabelle thought Kaitlyn gave good answers, but she could have shared a few more details.

When Mrs. Mitchell called on Annabelle, she was still thinking about Kaitlyn's response.

"Annabelle . . . Annabelle Copeland!" Mrs. Mitchell raised her voice a little louder the second time, so Annabelle finally snapped out of her thoughts.

"Yes, Mrs. Mitchell," Annabelle finally said.

"Welcome back to class," Mrs. Mitchell said with a smile. Some of the class couldn't help but laugh at Annabelle's daydreaming. "Are you ready to share your three most important things with us now?"

But what they didn't know about Annabelle is that she was always ready to give an appropriate response, even after daydreaming. She was born ready, at least according to her parents.

"I apologize for my over-thinking. I was really trying to focus on what was truly important to me. I wanted my answers to mean something. The three most important things about me are that I always speak my mind and am very truthful, I always do my best, and I will always strive to be my amazing self and have a positive attitude. Thank you," Annabelle said.

"Bravo! You go, girl!" Kaitlyn yelled out as she clapped her hands along with a few other students.

"Okay, class, that will be enough now," Mrs. Mitchell said, trying to quiet down the class. "That was a thoughtful response, Annabelle," Mrs. Mitchell said, clearly impressed.

The rest of the class continued to give their responses until the last student was finished. But it was very obvious that Annabelle's response really stood out. This fact made Annabelle feel warm inside.

"We have certainly learned a lot of interesting facts about each other this morning," Mrs. Mitchell said as she wrapped up the activity.

"But, Mrs. Mitchell," said Annabelle, "we're not finished yet. You forgot to tell us three important things about you."

The class agreed and urged Mrs. Mitchell to share too.

"Well, I'm so glad you asked. The three most important things about me are: first, I love to act and sing, and so I work role-playing and singing into my lessons," began Mrs. Mitchell.

"The next important thing is that I love teaching students new and exciting and amazing things."

Annabelle was ready to clap at that one.

Mrs. Mitchell continued, "And the last thing is I just love celebrations! We're actually going to celebrate a special topic in our curriculum every month!"

Annabelle was so excited along with the rest of the class. Mrs. Mitchell was already becoming the teacher of her dreams.

"So, what is our first celebration in September going to be, Mrs. Mitchell?" Annabelle asked.

"Why, an Apple Celebration of course! Now, I can't spill the beans about it just yet. We haven't even started our Science Apple Unit. We're going to save all that good stuff for next week," said Mrs. Mitchell, who was clearly excited about her plans.

Annabelle then remembered that she had packed an extra apple for the teacher in her backpack. She immediately jumped up and ran to the closet to get it. Everyone looked at Annabelle as if she had two heads. She quickly searched through her backpack, grabbed the apple, and eagerly ran up to the front of the room to give it to Mrs. Mitchell.

"This is for you, Mrs. Mitchell. I almost forgot that I had it until you mentioned the Apple Celebration!" Annabelle couldn't hide her excitement.

"Wow, what a pleasant surprise!" said Mrs. Mitchell as she accepted the gift. "And such a coincidence as well! It just so happens that apples are my favorite fruit! Thank you, Annabelle. That was very thoughtful of you."

"You're welcome," Annabelle said as she walked back to her desk, beaming with pride.

Annabelle happened to glance over at Sally for a quick second. She noticed that Sally was frowning and had a mean look in her eyes. But Annabelle didn't let Sally's actions bother her. Her mom had told her about mean-spirited people and jealousy. So, Annabelle just smiled at Sally as she sat down gracefully.

Annabelle had other amazing thoughts and ideas in her head about the

Apple Celebration. She couldn't wait to discuss her ideas with Kaitlyn.

"Just like I said, this year school's going to be the biggest adventure ever," Annabelle whispered under her breath.

4

APPLE RESEARCH PROJECT

The second week of school began, and Mrs. Mitchell started the science unit on the life cycle of apples. Annabelle decided to wear her favorite red apple dress to school on that day to welcome the occasion. Kaitlyn had a red outfit on too because they had talked about wearing the same color clothing to school on certain days.

Once again, Annabelle brought in another apple for Mrs. Mitchell and placed it on her desk. This was just one step in their major plan to have an awesome apple adventure. Annabelle had waited for this day for a whole week, and now it was "game on." As the students entered the classroom, everybody noticed Annabelle's dress right away.

"Will you get a load of her dress! Where on earth did you find that fashion disaster?" Sally asked in a loud voice.

"Maybe she found it at the apple farm on sale or something!" Jeanie said.

Some of the other kids laughed at the girls and made fun of them, but it didn't bother Annabelle, not one bit. Her amazingness was not going to be harmed by Jeanie or Sally. Annabelle decided to politely address the girls.

"Actually, my mom ordered this dress for me from a popular specialty store in New Zealand. She is always going online to find unique treasures for me. She knew I loved apples and surprised me with this amazing dress a while ago. So you see, it didn't come from an apple orchard as you have suggested. Beauty is in the eye of the beholder, and only special people can appreciate special things," Annabelle said confidently with a slight smile.

"It might be popular in New Zealand," said Sally, "but in America it just looks silly to me." Sally continued to laugh quietly as Annabelle took her seat.

"Special fashions are an acquired taste that some people will never understand or have," explained Annabelle in a matter-of-fact tone of voice.

"Whatever, Annabelle! You're giving me a headache!" Sally said, clearly frustrated at not being able to get her upset.

"I think your dress is really cool," Barry whispered to Annabelle.

Annabelle didn't even realize that Barry was paying attention to the conversation or her dress for that matter!

"Thank you," Annabelle whispered back gratefully.

Annabelle began to think about Barry's comment. She couldn't believe that Barry actually noticed her outfit or even cared about it. Ever since her family was invited to his pool over the summer, Annabelle really liked Barry as a good friend. Were things going to get more serious now? How serious could things possibly get, since they were just kids! Annabelle began to snap out of her daydream as Mrs. Mitchell addressed the class.

"Okay, boys and girls, as you know we're going to start our apple unit this week in science. We're going to learn about the life cycle of an apple. We are also going to visit an apple orchard to pick some delicious crunchy apples. After that, we will make apple cider and apple-sauce. Oh, and how could I forget our apple taste test! I hope that you are all as excited as I am for this awesome apple adventure!"

All the students stood up and cheered in response. Barry led the other students in a chant, "Ap-ples, ap-ples, ap-ples, ap-ples!"

Mrs. Mitchell quickly called for order. "Okay, boys and girls, let's settle down now. There's much work to be done."

Mrs. Mitchell took a clipboard from her desk as she continued, "Our first activity is a discovery research project on apples. I've divided the class into groups of threes. You'll work together to find out as much as you can about apples. You can create charts, graphs, and diagrams. Then your group must give all your data to the class in a special presentation. You'll have one week, and all your work must be done in class."

Annabelle thought this activity was the absolute best! This is what she had dreamed about. It was right up her alley.

She immediately opened her notebook and started making sketches of an apple tree. She even thought about writing a poem to go with the project.

Mrs. Mitchell looked at her clipboard and started dividing the class into groups. Annabelle wasn't paying attention until she heard her name called.

"Annabelle, David, and Sally; Kaitlyn, Barry, and Kara . . ." Mrs. Mitchell called out.

Annabelle thought for sure that there must have been some kind of mistake with the names. She raised her hand to speak.

"Yes, Annabelle?" Mrs. Mitchell asked.

Annabelle spoke quietly. "Can you

please call out the students in my group again? I didn't quite hear all the names."

Mrs. Mitchell was happy to help, and she looked at her clipboard again.

"Oh, sure," she said. "You're in the group with Sally and David."

"That's what I thought," Annabelle said, disappointed.

Oh, how she would have loved having Kaitlyn and Barry in her group! That would have been perfect.

As the students began to get together into their groups, Annabelle noticed Mrs. Mitchell alone at her desk, checking off things on her clipboard. Annabelle immediately went up to her before anyone else and began to speak to her in a soft voice.

"Mrs. Mitchell, would it be possible to switch into another group?"

Mrs. Mitchell looked concerned as she answered Annabelle.

"I've already made up the groups, and the students are beginning their assignment. Is there a problem I should know about?" Mrs. Mitchell asked.

Without getting too specific, she attempted to explain herself as she answered the question.

"Not exactly. Not right now. But there could definitely, potentially be a problem down the road somewhere, I think. I mean, Sally and I aren't exactly the best of friends these days," Annabelle said quietly.

Mrs. Mitchell was very understanding of Annabelle's situation and knew exactly how to respond to her.

"From what I know about you, Annabelle, I believe you can handle *any* problems or challenges that come up because you're a very smart and amazing girl. Now you go right over there and do what you do best. I have faith and confidence in you," the teacher said, gently patting Annabelle's arm.

A lightbulb went on in Annabelle's

mind. *Mrs. Mitchell is exactly right!* she thought. *I can do this!*

Annabelle looked over at Sally, who once again had a frown on her face. She knew this wasn't going to be easy, but she always welcomed a good challenge. Annabelle walked over to Sally and David with a big grin on her face.

5

PROBLEMS IN THE CHALLENGE

Annabelle was determined to be a light in what seemed to be a dark place. David wasn't really a problem—he just didn't talk that much. Annabelle honestly wasn't sure if he'd be able to pull his weight. Annabelle began to think that if she motivated and encouraged him enough, then maybe he could.

She knew her *real* problem was going to be Sally. *How do you work with a person who doesn't like you? Would Sally like her ideas? Would she just sit there with an attitude all day, not smiling or helping out?*

There's only one way to find out, Annabelle thought.

When Annabelle sat down at the desk with a positive attitude, she proceeded to ask questions to get an idea of what the other two were thinking.

"So what ideas did you two come up with for the activity?" Annabelle asked nicely.

David let out a long sigh and replied, "Nothing yet."

Sally rolled her eyes and said, "I'm still thinking."

This was going to be harder than Annabelle expected. But she was determined to break the ice and get things moving along. A lightbulb flickered in Annabelle's mind, and she immediately shared what she believed was an amazing idea.

"David, since you're such an excellent artist, why don't you draw a picture of the four seasons of an apple tree?"

David rubbed his head and then started nodding his head up and down with a happy look on his face.

"Okay, I can start working on that," he said. "Hey, maybe I could label the parts of the tree too."

"That's a great idea, David!" said Annabelle.

Now what bag of tricks could she suggest to Sally, who still had a frown on her face? Another idea popped in Annabelle's head just as quick as the first.

"Sally, since you're so good at research, why don't you Google the life cycle of an apple and see what other information you can find about it? Maybe you can make a diagram of the inside of an apple and then—"

Sally cut her off in an upset voice. "Who do you think you are giving orders to? You are *not* in charge of this group!"

Annabelle, who doesn't scare easily, answered quickly.

"I was just giving you a suggestion. How long are you going to sit at that

desk with a frown on your face? We *all* have to do some part of this project! I just wanted to kick things off, since you haven't suggested anything yet," said Annabelle.

"What part are you doing, little Ms. Know-it-all?" Sally asked in a singsong voice.

Sally was jealous of Annabelle's leadership and was teasing Annabelle because of it. Annabelle's mom had told her about mean-spirited people who just won't like you no matter how hard you try. Annabelle was quickly discovering that Sally might be one of those people.

For the first time in a long time, Annabelle wasn't feeling so amazing. At first, she didn't know how to respond to Sally.

Then Annabelle took a deep breath and answered Sally in the best way she knew how. "Since I'm a people person, I'm going to create a class apple chart and ask everyone in the class what their favorite kind of apple is—Granny Smith, Golden Delicious, or Red Delicious. I'm going to get started on that right away. And you can do whatever you like, just as long as you do something, instead of just sitting there," Annabelle said.

To her surprise, David commented, "That's a good idea, Annabelle!"

"Whatever!" Sally said, shrugging her shoulders.

Annabelle didn't speak with Sally for the rest of the day. Annabelle was upset. She had let Sally get to her, and as a result, she was disappointed with herself.

6

PEP TALK

On the bus ride home, Annabelle barely spoke a word. Kaitlyn could tell that she was still upset, so she tried to cheer Annabelle up as much as she could.

"I can't believe we got so much work done in our groups today. Mrs. Mitchell sure knows her stuff. I can't wait until tomorrow to finish working on this project," Kaitlyn said.

Annabelle didn't even crack a smile. She just stared out the bus window.

"I think I might be coming down with something," Annabelle finally said after a few coughs. "I don't know if I'm going to be in school tomorrow."

Annabelle had never been absent from school a day in her short life! She loved everything about school. Just being at school every day was like good medicine to her soul. Right then Kaitlyn became very concerned about Annabelle.

"Are you sure about that, Annabelle? You look fine to me," Kaitlyn said.

Annabelle let out a few more fake coughs as she answered Kaitlyn, "I think so."

Kaitlyn could always tell when Annabelle was faking.

"Look, Annabelle, you can't let Sally get to you like this. All she wants to do is make you feel bad because she doesn't like you. And so what if she doesn't like you! You have plenty of friends who *do* like you and know that you're an amazing person. I'm one of those people," Kaitlyn said to encourage her.

Annabelle knew at that moment that she had one of the very best friends in the whole wide world sitting right next to her. Annabelle finally cracked a little smile.

"Thank you, Kaitlyn, for those kind words." Annabelle was actually starting to feel a little better. Even her fake sickness was going away.

Just then, the bus came to a halt. It was Sally's stop. As she walked from the back seat to get off the bus, she made it her business to give Annabelle a frown and rolled her eyes at her. Annabelle glanced at her with a serious face and didn't move or blink, not even once. Annabelle was trying to regain her lost courage.

The next bus stop was Annabelle's.

She said bye to Kaitlyn and slowly got off the bus. Her brother pushed passed her and ran up to their house first. Annabelle had a lot to think about when she got home.

Annabelle's mom greeted her and Jason as they walked into the house. She noticed that Annabelle wasn't her normal, joyful self.

"So how was school today, Annabelle?" her mom asked.

Before Annabelle could even answer, her little brother loudly said, "Annabelle had a fight with Sally at school!"

Annabelle was shocked. *Where was this little kindergarten pest getting his information from? His response wasn't even close to the truth.* The false news certainly had spread quickly.

Annabelle quickly said, "That is *so* not true, Mom. He doesn't even know what he's talking about! Where are you getting your information from, anyway?"

Jason jokingly said, "Everyone was talking about it on the bus. Sally doesn't even like you!"

Annabelle couldn't believe the situation had gotten so far out of hand. Not knowing what else to do, Annabelle ran upstairs to her room crying. Jason stopped laughing and started to feel sad about what he had done and said.

"I didn't mean to make Annabelle sad, Mom. I'm sorry. I should have just kept my big mouth shut! Now Annabelle isn't going to ever talk to me again."

"I think you're being a little hard on yourself, Jason. Annabelle just needs a little time to think about things. I'm going to go upstairs and talk to her. But I'm sure she'd appreciate a little apology from you later," Mom said.

"Okay, Mom," Jason said as he went up to his room to start his homework.

Mom went upstairs and gently knocked on her daughter's door. Annabelle knew right away that it was her mom coming to talk with her. She faintly gave a response that her mom could barely hear. So Mom went in anyway and saw that Annabelle was lying on her bed. Mom sat down beside her and gently rubbed her back.

"Honey, what happened today at school?"

That was certainly a loaded question. Annabelle didn't know where to begin or how much to tell her. All she could say was how Sally was being so mean when she just made a suggestion to her. And if that weren't enough, Sally kept on making mean faces throughout the day and even on the bus.

"Mom, she just brought my spirits down," Annabelle said. "I tried to shake it off, but Sally was so mean to me over and over, all day long, like she was on a mission to hurt me."

Mom, in all her wisdom, gave Annabelle some solid advice.

"I see this situation really has you upset," Mom said as she tried to console her. "Sometimes we have to fight meanness, but we need to do it with kindness. Annabelle, you are a very kind and caring person. Don't let someone else stop you from being the amazing person you are inside your heart."

Mom continued, "Do some positive things and enjoy conversations with some of your other friends. Never return meanness to her. Just be positive and stand your ground. And always remember, you have the power to walk away from unpleasant situations."

Annabelle sat up on her bed and gave her mom a big hug. That was one of the best pep talks ever. Annabelle thought of her mom as her hero. She always knew the right things to say, no matter what the situation.

Annabelle felt recharged and ready for whatever situations came her way. Once again, Annabelle was smiling. Her amazingness was turned up to full power.

7

OPERATION KINDNESS

As Annabelle and Jason waited for the bus the next morning, Jason said the most unexpected thing to his sister. "Listen Annabelle, I'll deal with that Sally girl for you. I never liked her anyway!"

Annabelle couldn't believe the words that were coming out of his mouth! *Is this really my brother, or was he cloned by an alien last night and replaced while he slept?* she wondered. *And exactly how would Jason deal with her? What was going on inside that little head of his?*

Whatever he was thinking, Annabelle thought it was very nice of him to stand up for her. It's amazing what a little guilt will make you do. Annabelle could see the headline now: *The Copeland Kids: United in Teamwork Against the Meanness that Lingers Within the Bus.*

Annabelle had newfound confidence now, and she was cranking it up into high gear. She thanked Jason for his kind thoughts, no matter how unrealistic they were. Annabelle had devised a new plan she was going to put into action today called "Operation Kindness."

When the bus pulled up to their stop, Jason got on first, followed by Annabelle. She walked down the aisle and sat next to Kaitlyn as she always did. Kaitlyn smiled as she greeted her.

"Hi, Annabelle, I guess your cold is a lot better today," Kaitlyn joked.

"Hi, Kaitlyn. Yes, I'm feeling amazing today. My mom helped me refuel my energy tank, and I'm good to go." Annabelle smiled.

"I'm so happy to hear that," Kaitlyn said.

"I really want to thank you for yesterday on the bus. You said some pretty amazing things to me. I truly needed them. Thanks for being a great friend," Annabelle said with a smile.

"They don't call me Kindhearted Kaitlyn for nothing!" Kaitlyn and Annabelle began to laugh.

The bus pulled up at the next stop, which happened to be Sally's. She stepped onto the bus with the same frown she had worn yesterday.

As Sally walked down the aisle, Annabelle stopped laughing for a moment. She made it her business to say something to Sally.

"Hi, Sally," Annabelle said and didn't even wait for a response. She immediately went back to laughing and talking with Kaitlyn. Sally went on to her seat without saying a word back to Annabelle.

So far, so good. Operation Kindness is underway, Annabelle thought. There was no turning back now. When they arrived at school, everyone went to their individual classes, and everything began as normal.

Mrs. Mitchell announced that everyone would be meeting with their groups from yesterday to finish up the apple activities.

Annabelle forced a smile on her face and remembered what her mom told her yesterday about fighting meanness with kindness. Annabelle was determined to give it her best shot.

Just as all the students were getting into their groups from yesterday, David came running over to Annabelle. He held a big poster and looked excited.

"Hey, Annabelle, look at these drawings I did for each season of the apple tree!" he said.

David had done an amazing job on his poster. He even labeled the parts and colored them in with markers. David was very proud of himself. Annabelle couldn't wait to compliment him.

"David, you did an awesome job! You are the best artist I know. Mrs. Mitchell is going to love this. Your contribution to this group is priceless!"

Annabelle really gave him a lot of praise and encouragement.

David gave her a big smile and nodded happily as he sat down with the group, making finishing touches on his pictures. Annabelle noticed Sally working on a poster too. Annabelle couldn't believe it—she had actually listened to her idea! Sally had drawn a big diagram of the inside of an apple. She labeled the stem, flesh, core, seeds, skin, and leaves. Annabelle was so excited. She decided to give Sally a compliment as well.

"This is an awesome diagram, Sally! You have certainly captured the quality of an apple. I guess that Google search really helped you out. You are such a great artist," Annabelle said.

Sally responded quietly, "I guess."

Annabelle thought that was certainly a pleasant change. At least she didn't say anything negative or mean. Annabelle could definitely deal with that response.

She guessed being kind had actually worked, at least for now. The day wasn't finished yet, but Annabelle was very hopeful.

Annabelle continued working on her

class apple chart, which was turning out pretty amazing as well. She also was able to put the finishing touches on a poem about apples. Annabelle was beginning to think that this group thing wasn't so bad after all.

8

JOHNNY APPLESEED

The last day of the apple activities finally arrived. Mrs. Mitchell had promised the class a big surprise at the end of the week. Each group had to stand up in front of the class and give a report on what they did and what they learned. Annabelle and the other students hoped that wasn't the only surprise the teacher had for them. *What did Mrs. Mitchell have up her sleeve?* They would have to wait a bit to find out.

The first part of the morning began with apple presentations from each group. Of course, Annabelle wore her silk apple scarf and apple barrettes, which were the finishing touches to her whole outfit. Many of the students wore something with their favorite apple color on it, or something with some kind of apple theme. Kaitlyn's mom had brought her a pair of apple earrings, and David had on a green shirt.

But the surprise of the day was Sally. She wore a red apple shirt! Sally was really getting into the apple spirit today. She even looked friendly enough to talk with. Her usual frown was replaced with a kind smile. It seemed that the Good Apple Fairy had waved her magic wand over Sally. Annabelle walked over to pay her a compliment.

"Sally, that's an awesome apple shirt you have on! I know our group is going to do a great job on our presentation," Annabelle said.

"I think you're right about that," Sally responded with a smile.

Sally actually had a positive attitude today! David was pretty excited as well. Annabelle volunteered their group to go first.

Just as Annabelle expected, their group did great! David talked about the seasons of an apple tree and displayed his chart, and Sally discussed her apple diagram. And, of course, Annabelle concluded their presentation by sharing the results of her class apple graph and shared her poem, which went like this:

Apples

First you plant an apple seed.
Then you give it what it needs.
Water, air, and heat from the sun.
Then apple buds bloom one by one.

Pollination must happen
For the tree to bear fruit.
So many glorious blossoms!
They really look so cute!

So they're visited by bees,
Who do their job well.
They move into orchards,
And there, they dwell,
Until it's time to leave.

Then flower petals fall,
As apples begin to grow,
They bring joy to us all!
Red, yellow, green,
And mixtures too.
I really love apples!
How about you?

Everyone clapped for the group when they had finished. Writing poetry was a gift Annabelle really enjoyed sharing with others.

After all the groups gave their presentations, Mrs. Mitchell made a quick call on the school telephone in their room. Then she addressed the class.

"Well, you all did a magnificent job on your apple activities! I'm so proud of each and every one of you. I see this self-discovery activity really made the apple unit come alive. You have all learned a lot of valuable things that I know you won't forget."

Before Mrs. Mitchell could say anything else, Kaitlyn decided to interrupt her with a question.

"So, Mrs. Mitchell, what is the special apple surprise you promised us?" Kaitlyn asked.

A lot of the other class members began to chime in and ask about the big surprise. Mrs. Mitchell calmed the class down and continued with her speech.

"There is a very special visitor who'll be knocking on our door in just a few moments. This person really loves apples too. Long ago he used to travel from place to place planting apple seeds wherever he went. He planted lots and lots of apple trees in many different parts of the

world. Does anyone know who I'm talking about?" Mrs. Mitchell asked.

The class started to talk with each other to see if anyone could figure out who Mrs. Mitchell was talking about.

Barry decided he would give the answer a shot.

"Oh, I know, it was the Apple Genie who lived in a bottle!" Barry said and then laughed.

Many of the students laughed too. Mrs. Mitchell gave Barry a raised eyebrow that let him know that she didn't approve of his silly response.

Just then there was a knock on their classroom door. Mrs. Mitchell opened the door and to their amazement, in walked none other than Johnny Appleseed!

Of course the class noticed right away that it was Mr. Jefferson, the principal of the school. He was dressed in blue jeans, a white buttoned-down shirt, and he had a metal pot on his head as a cap. He was carrying a large sack of Red Delicious, Granny Smith, and Golden Delicious apples for the entire class!

"Now this is the best surprise ever!" Annabelle said.

Mr. Jefferson stayed for a short while and told the class the real story of Johnny Appleseed. The class hung on to his every word. They asked him all sorts of questions and had a detailed discussion of his life and adventures. When it was time for him to leave, the class clapped their hands and thanked him for bringing all the apples.

"So, Mrs. Mitchell, what are we going to do with all these apples?" David asked.

"Well, I guess we could cut a few of each kind and have a taste test," she said.

"Oh my goodness! That's the second best surprise ever!" Annabelle said.

As Mrs. Mitchell prepared the apples for the taste test, the class sang their apple songs and recited apple poems. Everyone tasted the three types of apples to see which kind was the class favorite, as Annabelle had done previously. Mrs. Mitchell graphed the responses. Red Delicious won hands down!

This was turning out to be such an awesome apple surprise. Everyone wondered what Mrs. Mitchell had planned for the afternoon.

9

STEPPING OUT OF THE COMFORT ZONE

During lunch, Annabelle, Kaitlyn, and Barry sat together in the cafeteria. Everyone was still talking about Mr. Jefferson walking around as Johnny Appleseed.

"I've never seen Mr. Jefferson wear jeans to school in my life! I thought jeans weren't allowed for teachers," Kaitlyn said.

"Yeah, he always wears the same boring black suit day after day," said Barry.

Of course, Annabelle was able to shed some light on the situation.

"It's a very special occasion today," she said. "I'm sure Mrs. Mitchell and Mr. Jefferson planned this whole thing together. I guess he can take one day off from wearing his boring suit to school. Although I have noticed that he often wears different ties."

Just then, in the middle of their conversation, Annabelle noticed Sally sitting at a lunch table by herself. She thought about walking over to start up a conversation. *But what if Sally is mean to me again? Should I just play it safe and stay at the table with my friends? What if Sally thinks I am treating her like a charity case? Maybe she just wants to be alone.*

Annabelle put all her negative thoughts aside and went for it. She excused herself from her table for a moment and walked over and sat next to Sally. She noticed Sally hadn't eaten her cup of peaches for lunch. Annabelle struck up a conversation by making a comment about the peaches.

"I couldn't eat my peaches either. I

prefer fresh fruit much more than canned fruit any day," Annabelle said.

"It just tastes really bad to me. I think the juice is a little sour," Sally said.

Could Annabelle and Sally really be bonding over a cup of canned peaches? Annabelle had stepped out of her comfort zone. She had been trying this Operation Kindness mission, and it seemed to be working.

"I think applesauce would have been the right kind of fruit choice today," Annabelle said.

"You can say that again," Sally said, now smiling.

Jokingly, Annabelle did just that. "I think some applesauce would have been the right kind of fruit choice today," Annabelle repeated.

They both start laughing at her silliness. Once again, Annabelle had broken the ice with Sally. They even were talking and playing outside during recess.

Annabelle was really starting to connect with Sally. She had never seen this side of Sally before. She seemed happy and fun to be with. Maybe Sally just wanted to take a break from having an attitude for a while. Maybe deep inside, she longed for a friend like Annabelle to play with her. Annabelle was starting to think that maybe Sally wasn't so bad after all.

10

APPLE CELEBRATION

After recess the students came into the classroom and were completely astonished by what they saw. Mrs. Mitchell had changed into an awesome apple dress with a matching hat and sandals! Annabelle wasn't the only one with good apple sense in dressing. She wondered if she had purchased it online from New Zealand as her mother had. Annabelle stood there, almost bewildered, looking at Mrs. Mitchell's outfit.

"That has to be the best apple dress I've ever seen! Where on earth did you get it from? I just have to get a hat like that one!" Annabelle said with excitement.

Mrs. Mitchell stood there in a model stance as she answered Annabelle. "Now, now, Annabelle, a teacher can't give up all her apple secrets. Some things must be left to the imagination."

Annabelle knew she wasn't going to spill the beans about her apple outfit, but she still thought it was outstanding. Annabelle actually felt proud to have Mrs. Mitchell as her teacher. She felt as if they were friends in a strange kind of way. They both shared the same love of snazzy dressing for special occasions. Annabelle liked Mrs. Mitchell's fashion style as well as her teaching style.

Each table in the classroom was now set up with big apple patterns, Popsicle sticks, buttons, felt materials, bottle caps, googly eyes, tissue paper, construction paper, stickers, crayons, markers, glue, scissors, and other decorations. On a U-shaped table in the back of the room, there were apple juice boxes, applesauce, apple chips, dried apples, and apple cupcakes. All the students stood looking around the room with excitement. Mrs. Mitchell began to explain everything to the class.

"Well, as we conclude our amazing apple activities, I just want to say that everyone did a great job! Right now, we're going to use the rest of the day to create our very own apple puppets, and then we're going to have a puppet theater!" Mrs. Mitchell said.

The whole class cheered loudly with excitement. She quieted the class down and continued.

"After we finish, we're going to have an apple delicious party with lots of apple treats! Who knows, maybe Johnny Appleseed will come in and join us again!"

This was definitely the icing on the cake—certainly a fun afternoon at school. Mrs. Mitchell allowed the students to work at whatever table they wanted to for this activity. Annabelle went up to Sally and acted quickly with her Operation Kindness mission.

"Hey, Sally, why don't you come and sit over here with Kaitlyn and me? We can all work together," said Annabelle.

Once again, Annabelle had gone out of her comfort zone. *Would Sally feel comfortable working with both girls? How does Kaitlyn feel about all of this? Would she be okay with it?* Before Annabelle could say anything else, Sally spoke hesitantly.

"Sure, I guess," she said and went over to their table. Kaitlyn welcomed Sally with a big smile. Each of the girls decorated and talked, laughing and enjoying each other's company.

When it was time for the puppet theater presentations, two or three students got together behind the curtain and had funny conversations. Each student gave their apple puppet a different name and shared what kind of fake job they had. Or they talked about things their apple puppet liked to do. Most of the time it was just silly talk that made the class laugh.

Even Mrs. Mitchell made an apple puppet and participated. She was the first puppeteer to perform, so she could show everyone else how it was supposed to be done.

She named her apple puppet Princess Mary Macintosh, Queen of the Library. Mrs. Mitchell was very active, changing her voice as she spoke. She told a short story of how the princess had to rescue stolen library books from an evil cat. The students were hanging on to her every word. Of course, the story had a happy ending, and the apple princess lived happily ever after. The class clapped for her excellent story.

Next up was Annabelle, Kaitlyn, and Sally. They pretended their apple puppets were three good friends who did everything together. Little did they know just how true to life their theme would become.

After everyone had their chance to shine in the puppet theater, it was time to enjoy all the delicious apple treats Mrs. Mitchell had prepared for the class. She put on a cool music video for the kids to watch as everyone ate their special treats. Some students even stood up and did a little dancing with the video.

This was the best day of school yet, and the school year had just begun! The beginning of the year had brought a new and unexpected friendship for Annabelle. She was branching out and connecting with another person through Operation Kindness, and that made Annabelle feel good inside.

The Apple Celebration was such a great event for the month of September. Annabelle couldn't wait to see what was on the agenda for next month.

ANNABELLE'S DISCUSSION CORNER

1. In Chapter Three, Annabelle and her classmates had to introduce themselves to the class. List three important things that are special about you and why.

2. In Chapter Five, Sally was teasing Annabelle. How would you feel if someone were teasing you, and what are some things you could do to make the situation better?

3. What is your favorite food made with apples?

Don't miss Annabelle's other amazing books!

Amazing Annabelle and the Fall Festival

Amazing Annabelle—Thank You, Veterans

Amazing Annabelle and December Holidays and Celebrations

ABOUT THE AUTHOR

 Linda Taylor has been teaching students for over 25 years. She enjoys connecting with students on many levels. She also loves writing poetry. Linda lives on Long Island, New York.

ABOUT THE ILLUSTRATOR

 Kyle Horne has a B.A. in Visual Communications from S.U.N.Y. Old Westbury College in New York. Kyle has displayed his artwork in many local libraries. He lives on Long Island.